THE LOST ISLAND

AYLA HASHWAY

↑
author

Diya
kaur

↑
reader

THE LOST
Island

AYLA HASHWAY

DEDICATION

To my fans, family, and fourth grade class.

TABLE OF CONTENTS

From Bad to Worse

Chapter Fifteen
Looking For Revenge

Chapter Sixteen
Trading Tricks

CHAPTER ONE
SECRET DISCOVERY

As twelve-year-old Olivia Lockhart watched Aunt Amanda fly away in the helicopter, she still could not believe what had happened over the past few weeks. Like how Aunt Amanda had dressed up in different disguises to lure Olivia to Abura and kidnapped her family all to steal Olivia's inventions and ideas.

Olivia looked down at her empty hands with a sad look on her face.

Olivia's mother looked down at Olivia. "What happened, kiddo?" she asked.

"She took my invention notebook with her when she escaped," Olivia said with tears in her eyes.

"Oh, I'm sorry, honey," her mom said.

"It was all my fault," Olivia said quietly. "I was the one who forgot to take the notebook and let her get away."

"It was all of our faults," said her dad.

"But I was the one who fell for her tricks," Olivia said with an ashamed look on her face and a little surprised that her parents weren't mad at her. "After all, I was the one who said that we should go to Abura."

Her mom sighed. "I should have told you guys

about her," her mom said, looking down at Olivia and Max.

"Um, Mom, about that..." Olivia started to say.

Max elbowed her in the arm.

"What is it now?" Olivia asked in a loud whisper.

"Are you really going to tell her?" Max whispered back.

"What are you two talking about?" their mom asked them.

"Yes, I have to, Max," Olivia insisted.

"Oh, okay!" Max said a little too joyfully. "Olivia was the one who said we should reverse the tracker on her phone to track you down and find out where you were going. And then we found out about Aunt Amanda *way* before you knew."

"What? Max!" Olivia said, unable to believe that Max just said that. Well, it wasn't fully unbelievable.

"Wait. What? Is that true?" Mom asked.

"Well, yeah, kind of," Olivia said, looking at her mom. "I'm really sorry. Plus, Max helped."

"Next time, please tell me when you do those kinds of things," their mom replied, not in a very happy voice, though. "By the way, the both of you are grounded when we get home from vacation."

"But..." Max started to say.

"No, you're both grounded, and that is final."

Max crossed his arms and started to pout. "How long is Olivia grounded?" he asked.

"Max, she said the both of us," Olivia said while rolling her eyes.

"You are *both* grounded for two weeks," their father said in a stern voice.

"What?" Max cried. "Two weeks?"

"Well, Olivia should only be grounded for one week since she freed us," their mom said.

"Yes!" Olivia said, jumping up and down.

"Hear that, Olivia? I'm only grounded for one week, and you're stuck with two. Ha!" Max said, sticking his tongue out at Olivia.

"Um, Max, Olivia is grounded for only one week. *You* are grounded for *two* weeks," Mom said.

"Fine, but I will get my revenge!" Max screamed.

"So, how come you never told me about your sister?" Dad asked Mom. "You owe me an apology."

"Um, no. I don't owe you anything after you bought that fishing boat without even asking for my opinion first!" Mom said in a stern voice.

"Not that again. And yes, you do!" Dad argued back.

"No, don't even get me started!" Mom yelled.

Olivia always hated when her parents fought. It was like her parents had forgotten what had just happened a couple of minutes ago with Aunt Amanda.

Olivia took a step back. Watching her parents act like this made Olivia feel like they might divorce one day. Olivia tried not to think about it, but she couldn't stop.

"Ha-ha, ha-ha!" Max laughed.

Olivia and Max had very different points of view. Olivia took things seriously, didn't fool around a lot, always worried about disasters that could happen, and thought logically or realistically about things.

Max, on the other hand, always was trying to get out of trouble, laughed when things were rough between Mom and Dad, never took anything seriously, and rarely ever listened.

Sometimes Olivia wished she were an only child. Max was always in the way of things. Olivia was a straight A+ student, but it was very difficult to concentrate with Max around.

Olivia turned around and sat on the couch, going through her invention bag. Suddenly, a book on the coffee table caught her eye. Olivia reached forward and grabbed the book from the table.

When she started to read in her head, Max turned around, not laughing anymore. He walked over and sat next to Olivia.

"So, what are you reading?" Max asked, looking over Olivia's shoulder.

"I found this book on the table. It's about famous inventors and inventions. It even says it has some suggestions for inventions to make. No wonder Aunt Amanda needed this," Olivia replied.

Then their parents finally stopped arguing. "We are sorry for fighting. We didn't want to stress you guys out," their mom said, putting her arms around Olivia and Max.

"Well, now we know how you feel when you have to listen to us arguing," Olivia said with a chuckle.

"I still wish I had told you guys sooner," Mom said, looking at the ground. "Amanda wouldn't have gotten away."

"True. You should call the cops now," Max interrupted.

"I'll get on that right now, okay?" she said, taking her phone from the TV stand, where Aunt Amanda had left it after locking them up.

"Okay, I guess I'm in charge this time," Max said, standing up.

"Um, Dad is still here, you know," Olivia said, gesturing toward their father.

Max pouted. "I never win."

"Win what?" asked Olivia.

"Ugh, you know what I mean," Max said, his face turning bright red.

Olivia stifled a giggle. She turned around only to see her mom talking to the cops. Olivia frowned.

"What is wrong, honey?" Dad asked. "Something seems to be bothering you all of a sudden."

"You guys always trust the cops with things, and you never ask me to investigate at all or try to catch Aunt Amanda!" Olivia felt like she just let her heart explode. "Please just let me try again. There has to be something I'm missing about this place."

"Okay, my little detective," their dad replied. "But be safe. Max, you should go with your sister to investigate the rest of this place in case anything bad happens."

"Come on, Max! I don't want to wait any longer!" Olivia said a little bit too joyfully.

"Fine. I really hope this doesn't turn out to be useless like every other time I've helped you do something," Max groaned while trying to catch up to Olivia, who was already running down the hall.

"Come on, Max. I don't have time to waste waiting for you!" Olivia called from the end of the hall.

When Max caught up to Olivia, she was already

investigating the banner hanging in front of the secret passageway.

"You brought the other half of the star necklace?" Max asked halfheartedly. "Why would you want to remember Aunt Amanda?"

"I just don't want to lose it. That's all," Olivia said.

"Can I see it?" Max asked, tugging it out of Olivia's hand before she could answer him.

"Just be careful with that!" Olivia said as the necklace fell out of Max's hand and hit the shag carpet. "Max!"

"Yes?" Max asked in a worried voice.

Olivia tried to pick up the necklace, but she couldn't. It was caught on the carpeting.

"Weakling!" Max mocked as he watched Olivia trying to tug the necklace free.

"You try then!" Olivia said in an impatient and irritated voice.

"No problem," Max said in a self-confident voice.

Max pulled, but it was no use. Max tugged again, but he ended up rolling backward into the wall. "Ouch!" Max yelped.

"Get over it, you big baby!" Olivia said.

"You try again. I need a break," Max said, acting as if he were about to die.

"Fine," Olivia replied.

When Olivia tugged this time, the piece of carpeting the necklace was stuck to all of a sudden flapped up to reveal an underground lair.

Would Olivia finally get what she wanted and catch Aunt Amanda?

CHAPTER TWO
THE UNDERGROUND LAIR

O livia and Max stared down into the underground lair in shock.

"Whoa!" Olivia and Max both said in unison. Their eyes were bulging. They were amazed at what they were seeing.

"Do you think Aunt Amanda knows about this place?" Max asked.

Olivia gave him a look. "Really? Of course, she knows about it. There is one of her company flyers on that desk!" Olivia said, pointing to the flyer on the wooden desk.

"I-I knew that," Max said, waving his hand in the air.

Olivia could tell that Max was lying to her and he didn't really know that. "Sure, let's go with that," Olivia said and rolled her eyes.

"The underground lair seems really far down," Max said, trying to change the subject. "There aren't even stairs or an elevator!"

"So?" Olivia said as her sneaker slipped back.

"Olivia!" Max yelled, putting his hand out. "Look out!"

"Ahhh!" Olivia screamed.

When she had looked behind her, her foot had

slipped backward, making her fall backward and down into the lair.

"Are you okay?" Max yelled down, but it didn't really sound like he cared the least bit.

"Not really. There is hard concrete for the flooring!" Olivia answered.

"Ahhh!" Max yelled as he jumped down into the underground lair and onto the concrete flooring.

"Why on earth would you jump down here?" Olivia asked, watching Max lie on the ground in pain.

"I wanted to see what it is like down here," Max said in a muffled voice.

"You should have called Mom and Dad to help me get out of here or tell them what happened and that I am going to investigate!" Olivia complained. "But no. You just had to jump so you could see what it is like down here, and because of that, we might be stuck down here forever!"

"First of all, how would I call Mom or Dad if I don't have a phone?" Max asked.

"You know what I mean!" Olivia said. "You are just jealous that I have a phone and you don't!"

"Second of all, we will die eventually, so we can't live here forever," Max couldn't help but say.

"You are right. I would die. If I were stuck in a

room with you for even a day, I *would* die!" Olivia fought back.

"We could just yell to Mom and Dad, you know," Max suggested.

"Sure, that will work," Olivia said sarcastically.

"Can we just try? It's better than doing nothing and being stuck down here forever," Max said.

"*We can't stay down here forever. We would die!*" Olivia mimicked Max from earlier when she had said the same thing.

"Hey!" Max yelled.

"Oh, quit acting like I have never done anything like that before!" Olivia said, acting like it was nothing.

"Let's just try yelling," Max begged. "Please!"

"Fine!" Olivia snapped.

"Yes!" Max said, jumping up and down.

"Calm down, pip-squeak!" Olivia said, getting tired of listening to him yap.

"Ready?" Max asked.

"Sure, why not?" Olivia answered.

"Mom, Dad, we are down here! Help!" they screamed in unison.

No answer.

"Let's try again!" Max said. "And let's scream louder this time. Okay?"

"All right!" Olivia agreed.

"Mom, Dad, we are down here! Help!" they tried again.

No answer. Just a moment of silence.

"Did we do something wrong?" Max asked.

"Yes, we took your advice!" Olivia yelled.

"Well, do you have any ideas?" Max argued.

"Not at this very moment," Olivia said.

"Then I'd like to see you do better!" Max said back.

"Quiet. I'm thinking!" Olivia said, trying to get Max to stop talking so she could concentrate.

"Fine!" Max yelled.

"Fine!" Olivia mocked.

Max stuck his tongue out at Olivia.

"Wow, Aunt Amanda sure put a lot of effort into this place," Olivia said, practically touching everything in sight.

"Be careful. You don't know if she set any traps in here," Max warned.

"Max, come look at this!" Olivia exclaimed, unable to believe her eyes.

"Ugh! What now?" Max asked, trying to work his way to the back of the room where Olivia was.

"Look!" Olivia said.

"Look at what?" Max asked.

"Those are my inventions!" Olivia screamed. "Aunt Amanda made some of them by using the tools and parts from my invention bag!"

"I don't blame her. These are cool!" Max said. "I mean, for something you made, I guess."

"And look. There is my invention notebook!" Olivia exclaimed. "Wait, my invention notebook? That can't be possible!"

"Dun, dun, dun!" Max said in a mysterious voice.

"Max, quit fooling around!" Olivia said seriously. "I'm not kidding. I think she might have made a fake one to take with her when she escaped so she could lure us to her again!"

Olivia walked over to the notebook and opened it.

"Is it yours?" Max asked.

Olivia hesitated for a moment before saying, "No, Aunt Amanda has *my* invention notebook!"

"Then, let's get out of here," Max said. "Before Aunt Amanda gets too far away!"

"But that would mean us falling into her traps once again," Olivia said.

"How do you *know* that?" Max asked.

"Well I don't *know*," Olivia replied. "Plus, do you really think that she would just randomly leave in a helicopter and not know where she was going?"

"You never know," Max said. "I kind of would, but that is just me."

"She probably has a different hideout that she went to," Olivia said.

"I knew that," Max said.

Olivia rolled her eyes. "We better get out of here," she said.

"How?" Max asked. "There's only one exit, and it is useless! Useless! Useless! Useless!"

"Calm down. I'm sure there is another way out," Olivia said confidently. "At least, I sure hope so," she mumbled under her breath.

"Look over there!" Max exclaimed. "I think that's a door."

"Where?" Olivia asked, surprised that Max might have found something already. She'd been sure it would take him one million years to find another way out.

"Over there in that corner by the fake knight," Max explained.

Olivia walked over to the corner where the suit of armor stood. "There's a keyhole! We need to find the key first," Olivia explained.

"Where would we find a key around here? This place is a complete mess." Max complained.

"Funny how you notice this place is a mess when

your side of the room is a pigsty," Olivia pointed out.

Max just stood still in the middle of the room. "My side of the room is a masterpiece. If you had any artistic vision, you would see that," Max tried to explain in a way that was much more believable than other lies he had told in the past.

"Let's get back to work on trying to find the key so we can hopefully get out of here." Olivia was already rummaging through piles of junk on the old wooden table.

"Okay, fine," Max moaned. "I'll do anything to get away from you."

While they were looking through piles of papers, books, and inventions, Olivia and Max heard a loud screech. It almost sounded like metal rubbing against metal.

"What was that?" Max asked, startled by the noise. "Do you think it was a ghost?" Max started to shake and whimper.

"It's nothing!" Olivia stated. "Or it is the floor above us creaking."

All of a sudden something screeched again. The air in the room started to get colder and colder. It almost seemed as if they were in a horror movie. Then out of nowhere, the floor panel that Olivia was standing on broke and fell down to a lower level, almost taking Olivia with it.

"Ahhh!" Olivia screamed. Quickly, Olivia grabbed on to the edge of the panel closest to her with one hand. "Help, Max!"

"Huh?" Max asked, turning around to see Olivia dangling on a floor panel with one hand. "Lift your other arm up, and grab hold of the other panel. Then pull yourself up," Max explained, acting as if it were really nothing.

"It really isn't as easy as you truly think it is," Olivia explained to Max as she continued to struggle to pull herself up.

"Oh, look there's a rope on the wall over there!" Max stated. "Maybe we can throw it up on the level Mom and Dad are on. Then we can climb up to safety! I'm a genius!"

"Yeah, except I'm still down here dangling and holding on for dear life," Olivia pointed out, glaring at Max. "Maybe you could throw down the one end of the rope, I'll hold on, and you can pull me up."

"Or we could do that—if you want to do it the boring way," Max grumbled in disappointment.

"Ugh, just hurry up. I can't hang down here forever!" Olivia said, her face getting as red as a rose.

Max hurried over and grabbed the old, rusty rope.

He ran back to Olivia and threw one of the ends down to Olivia's hand that wasn't holding on.

"Is the rope going to break? It looks kind of fragile to me," Olivia pointed out. "I mean, I might be wrong, but it looks to me like that thing is way too old and frayed to help pull a twelve-year-old to safety in a crazy woman's underground hideout in her laboratory."

"It's fine. You are overreacting," Max said. "At least, I hope it's fine," Max mumbled to himself.

"Wait. What did you just say?" Olivia asked suspiciously.

"Ugh, you know, it is nothing. Just grab the rope all ready," Max said, covering what he had just said.

Still unsure, Olivia grabbed the rope with both hands. "Pull!" she said.

"Look! There is the key to the door. It's in the knight's hand!" Max exclaimed.

"Max!" Olivia yelled as Max let go of the old rope, making her fall to the ground.

Max didn't listen. He ran over and grabbed the key from the knight's hand and ran back to Olivia. "What happened?" Max asked. "You were supposed to hang on to the rope!"

"*I* held on to the rope. *You* were the one who let go to go get the key, and now that I'm down here, it will take even longer to get out," Olivia explained.

"I'm sorry but—" Max started to say.

"Max, watch out!" Olivia interrupted.

All of a sudden, the knight that was in the corner started walking toward Max. Then the knight put his hand on Max's shoulder.

"Ahhh!" Max screamed, terrified.

Would Olivia and Max ever make it out now?

CHAPTER THREE

ANOTHER SECRET

Instantly, Max jumped down into the underground lair Olivia was in.

"Ouch!" Olivia exclaimed. "Max, why in the world would you decide to jump down here?"

"I was scared, and I couldn't have escaped that knight if I didn't jump," Max tried to explain while getting off of Olivia, whom he had fallen on top of when he jumped.

"Ugh, I think you broke my hip bone," Olivia groaned. "Speaking of the knight, what are we going to do about him?" she shouted.

"Are you actually scared of me?" an unfamiliar voice asked.

"Was that a ghost talking?" Max said, jumping into Olivia's arms.

"Really?" Olivia asked, looking rather annoyed. "If anything, it is the knight-guy-thing talking."

"Yup, that's me up here," the knight said. "You know, that scary 'knight-guy- thing,'" he said, quoting what Olivia had called him.

Olivia dropped Max to the ground. "See, it's not a ghost, dummy," she said, rolling her eyes.

"You're right. It is worse!" Max shrieked.

"Relax. I'm not going to hurt you or anything," the knight explained. "I'm Rick Miller the third."

"I'm Olivia, and this is my little brother, Max," Olivia said, introducing herself.

"Pleasure to meet your acquaintance, Miss Olivia," Rick said charmingly. "I find it rather intriguing that you and your little brother get along so well."

"Not always," Olivia replied. "Actually, we barely ever get along."

"Why do you always call me 'little brother'?" Max complained.

"Really, you complain about everything. Now it's about being called little brother!" Olivia argued. "You were fine with it a couple days ago!"

"Well, now I'm not," Max said. "I am growing up, you know. You can even start calling me a man."

"Ugh," Olivia sighed and rolled her eyes. "It doesn't work that way!"

"Um, sorry to interrupt, but do you need help?" Rick asked. "It doesn't look like there is much room down there."

"Anything to get away from her," Max replied.

"Sure, thanks for your help by the way," Olivia said, looking over and glaring at Max.

Rick went to the middle of the room and picked up the rope they had used earlier. Rick looked at the rope a little confused. "This rope was fine when I got here," he said. "It wasn't old or frayed at all. What year is it?"

"It's 2017. Why?" Olivia answered.

"What? I have been down here for seven years?" Rick asked himself. "That can't be true."

"Seven years?" Max asked as Rick lowered the rope down to them.

After Olivia climbed up, she stood and brushed the dirt off her shirt. "Thank you for helping us up," she said. "But what exactly do you mean by seven years?"

"Oh, I have been guarding this place for years now," Rick explained.

"By choice?" Max asked, getting to the top.

"No. I work for Amanda Walters. Do you know her?" Rick asked.

"Yes, as a matter of fact we do," Olivia answered. "She is my evil secret aunt all right."

"Well, I was looking for a job one day, and I had started to give up, so I walked through the darkest, scariest place of all time—The Dark Forest—hoping it would get my life over with because I was poor and had no home or anything. Then I heard strange noises and followed them to the waterfall. Amanda offered me a job working for her, and I immediately said yes, not knowing she would only feed me once a week. I was kept down here for years. I was forgotten. I tried to escape. I have hated her so much ever since. I have wanted to get back at her, but if you haven't noticed, it is kind of hard to move in this armor. I wanted to come over to you when you first saw me, but my armor here wouldn't let me," Rick explained.

"So you have had a terrible experience with her, too," Olivia said. "Maybe after we get out of here, we can take you with us to go and eat."

"That would be great!" Rick said. "By the way, what happened to you guys and Amanda?"

"Oh boy, you better get comfy," Olivia warned.

"Well, I don't have anything better to do," Rick replied.

"For starters, she lured us here and captured my family and—" Olivia started to say before Max cut her off.

"We don't want to bore the man!" Max exclaimed.

"Max, he asked. I didn't just start babbling on and on about what she had done to us!" Olivia argued.

"You were still babbling if you think about it," Max said.

"Um, this might be a bad time to ask, but do you guys need help getting out of here?" Rick asked.

"Oh, yeah," Olivia remembered. "Thanks for reminding me."

Olivia grabbed her invention bag and started collecting items, like her inventions Aunt Amanda had made. She even took her fake invention notebook, some flyers from Aunt Amanda's business, some inventing supplies, and some other stuff that looked like gadgets and potions she figured she could use someday.

"Okay, if you are going to take everything, we might as well bring this whole place with us," Max said, getting impatient.

"I am not taking everything, so would you just chill?" Olivia answered.

"Fine, if you aren't taking everything, then can we get out of here and eat already?" Max asked.

"I am almost done," Olivia stated. "What do you think this thing is?" she asked, holding up a bottle of some green goo.

"What do I think what is?" Max asked, turning around only to see the green blob hanging directly in front of him.

"You know, this green stuff," she replied, shaking the glob in its jar.

"What's on the label?" Rick asked.

"It says 'Power Potion,' and then below it says

'Caution, there is no saying what power is inside," Olivia read off the label. "That makes no sense."

"I think you are supposed to eat it to get a power of some sort," Max said.

"I agree with him," Rick said, nodding.

"Ew, I would never eat that," Olivia said, backing away from it and cringing.

"I would eat it. I mean, who knows what power it holds," Max stated.

"Apparently not even its creator, Aunt Amanda," Olivia pointed out.

"Are you taking anymore, or can we be on our way?" Rick asked. "I'm starving."

"I feel you," said Max, rubbing his belly.

"No you don't, Max. He hasn't eaten in weeks!" Olivia replied. "You, on the other hand, have."

"So? Wouldn't he be pretty *dead* by now?" Max asked.

"I mean a full meal," Olivia stated. "Now let's get out of here after I get one more thing."

"Hurry up then," Max complained.

"No, you heard me wrong. We can get out of this room, but I need to grab something that's upstairs," Olivia corrected.

"Here. Give me the key. I'll unlock the door," Rick offered. "Unless you want to stay, of course."

"I'll pass. I do not want to stay here," Max said, putting his hand on his stomach.

Rick started walking toward the door in the corner while Olivia and Max followed him.

"After you," Rick said, holding the door for Olivia and Max.

Behind the door were weapons beyond belief. There was a whiteboard in the corner of the room that had Aunt Amanda's plan to get Olivia to Abura on it. Olivia reached for a cabinet door handle, but before she could, she was slapped away by Rick.

"Sorry, but I wouldn't touch that if I were you. They have a security system," Rick warned.

"What kind of security system?" Olivia asked, examining the cabinet.

"Well, it opens with a fingerprint. The scanner is on the side, but if you go to open it normally... Well, let's just say you'll get electrocuted and possibly die," Rick explained.

Olivia backed away and kept following Rick. "Um, where are we going? There's a dead end."

"Don't be fooled by her tricks," Rick said, pulling a lamp on the wall toward him.

The wall suddenly started to turn, but to Olivia's surprise, it stopped halfway. Rick stepped into one part of the contraption and waited for Olivia and Max to follow.

"I wouldn't trust him, Olivia," Max whispered.

Olivia ignored Max and followed Rick into the room. Before her stood a large staircase with a door at the top.

"Come on, Max. It's just a staircase. I think we can trust him," Olivia answered finally.

"What's behind the door?" Max asked.

"Wait and see," Olivia said, getting annoyed with Max for always doubting Rick.

Once they were up the staircase, Rick lifted a sign on the door to uncover another scanner. He put his hand over it and said the same password used on the door for the jail cell room. Rick put his arm out and stepped back, pushing Olivia and Max back with him. Slowly, the wall turned again. This time, they were back by the end of the hall where the banner was. Olivia and Max stepped through along with Rick. Olivia walked over to the piece of carpet that was still lifted up with her necklace attached to it. She tugged the necklace out from the piece of carpet and pushed the carpet back down to match the rest of the floor again.

"Olivia? Max? Is that you?" Mom asked from the sitting area.

"Um, yeah. Why?" Olivia asked, walking over to her mom and dad.

"Well, for a while, I was worried because—" Olivia's mom stopped when she saw Rick in the knight armor. "Who is that?" She quickly grabbed Olivia and Max and pulled them close to her.

Max shook out of his mom's grasp. "It's just Rick. Don't worry," he said, waving his hand in the air.

Olivia rolled her eyes at how Max now trusted Rick. "He was Aunt Amanda's slave," Olivia stated. "Don't worry. He's on our side."

"Side?" Mom asked. "What side?"

"He would do anything to get back at Aunt Amanda," Olivia said. "Can he come stay with us?"

Their mom looked at their dad in question. When Dad nodded, Mom said, "I suppose, but I will have to get to know him a little more."

"Thanks!" Olivia exclaimed, hugging her mom.

"Can we go eat now?" Max groaned.

"Sure. I saw a gelato place along the boardwalk by Scala's."

"What's Scala's?" Max asked.

"Another restaurant by the I Heart Abura store," Mom said. "But you kids can decide where you want to eat."

Olivia and Max looked at each other and nodded. "Gelato," they both said in unison.

"Well, then is that okay with you, Rick?" Dad asked.

"Sure. Any real food is better than what You Know Who gave me," Rick explained.

"Well, then it's settled," Mom said. "Gelato, here we come."

Rick started to get his knight armor off so he'd look and move like a normal person again.

"Let's go!" Max complained.

"Fine. Are you ready, Olivia?" Dad asked.

"Yup," Olivia said, grabbing the book of inventors off the table.

When they finally left and got through the creepy forest, Olivia sighed with relief. It was already dark, so they tried to get to the gelato place as soon as possible.

When they got there, Max was already in heaven looking through the window at all the flavors.

Olivia noticed that her mom was already on her phone. "What are you doing?" she asked, looking over her mom's shoulder.

Her mom jerked away, startled. "Um...nothing. Just um...texting Grandma to meet us here," her mom said.

Olivia didn't believe it for a second, especially when she heard her mom press the home button and go to Grandma in the contacts. Was her mom really lying to her again? She thought her mom was past that.

Olivia rushed over to Max and grabbed his arm. Then she pulled him away from the window so he would pay attention.

"Max, you will never believe this. Mom just..." Olivia started to whisper when Max cut in.

"What? Lied again?" Max asked.

"No, she...well, yes. How did you know?" Olivia asked a little confused that Max actually guessed correctly.

"Really? I was just kidding about that," Max said and then shrugged and asked, "So, what did she lie about this time?"

"Well, she said she was telling Grandma to meet us here, but then she went to her home screen and went to message Grandma," Olivia said in a rather loud whisper. "She's obviously hiding something from us again."

"Okay, how about we figure this out in the morning? I need to eat and go to bed."

"Fine," Olivia said.

Once they found the flavors they wanted, they

ordered and sat down at a table. The seating area was outside with fences bordering on two sides and a rope around the others. Olivia looked at the lit up buildings and a colorful water show with music across the street. Venders were surrounding the boardwalks and street.

"I say tomorrow we go after Aunt Amanda," Olivia said.

"No, you two are not going to hunt Aunt Amanda down. It's too dangerous," Mom insisted.

"Mom, of course we aren't going to hunt her down. We will track her down," Olivia said. "We are not monsters."

"My decision is final, Olivia, and by the way, that goes for you too, Max."

"What did I do?" Max asked.

"Fine. We will not go." Olivia crossed her arms.

She started taking in the view again when she saw a girl who looked around her age spying on her. Olivia got out of her seat, and the girl ran away.

Olivia ran after her. Unfortunately, when she went to cross the road, the cars blocked her, so she lost track of the girl by the time the cars passed.

When she headed back, her parents and Max were walking toward her along with Rick.

"What was that about?" her mom asked.

"Um, I wanted to get a better look at the water show, but the cars are blocking my view. Oh well," Olivia lied.

"Next time, tell us where you are going. You had us worried sick," their dad said.

"Sorry. I'll be more mindful next time," Olivia apologized.

They all headed back when Olivia's grandparents arrived. While Olivia's parents went to greet them, she kept Max and Rick aside.

"Listen, I lied, but I have to tell you the truth later."

CHAPTER FOUR

A FAMILIAR STRANGER

The next morning, Olivia awoke to a pillow in her face.

"So now how does it feel to wake up to a pillow being thrown in your face?" Max asked.

"Max, quit fooling around. Before Mom and Dad wake up, I need to tell you and Rick what happened last night."

They went downstairs to their penthouse living room. Rick was sleeping on the black couch. Max went over, took a pillow off a chair, and threw it at Rick.

"Max! Why would you throw a pillow at him?" Olivia scolded him in a loud whisper.

"Wow, that is not how I expected to be woken up in the morning, but I guess it's still better than waking up locked in an underground lair with no food," Rick complained in a tired voice as he sat up.

"Sorry about that. Max doesn't have any manners," Olivia said, glaring at Max.

"Well, his manners are better than Amanda's," Rick said.

"So, just tell us already what happened last night," Max yelled.

Olivia covered Max's mouth. "Max, would you be quiet? Mom and Dad are still sleeping."

"So, what exactly did happen? Why would you lie to your parents?" Rick asked a little confused.

"While we were eating at the gelato place last night, I saw this girl around my age spying on us. I wanted to chase after her to see what she was up to, but when the cars were passing, I lost sight of her. So when I started to head back, I had to make up a lie because Mom would have been all mad at me because I went after something that could have been dangerous."

"Yes, because a twelve-year-old girl is very dangerous," Max said.

"Well, I didn't know her. Mom and Dad don't want us talking to strangers. It's bad enough we can't even go after Aunt Amanda, who we know."

"Let me get this straight. You decided to chase after a random girl because she was looking at you?" Rick asked.

"Well, the girl was in the bushes with binoculars, and they were pointed right at us. I think she was spying," Olivia said, daring them to argue with that logic.

"Still, how do you know it was directly at us?" Max asked. "It might have been different from her point of view."

"Then why would she run when I went right toward her? It makes no sense, your logic, Max."

"I still don't know why you'd go right toward her," Max said, walking over to the other end of the room and skipping back over to Rick. "'Oh, hi, random stranger. Who are you spying on? I'm Olivia.' Blah, blah, blah. Make up all the excuses you want. She was a girl hiding in the bushes. She's a creep."

"And so was Aunt Amanda," Olivia whispered in a loud tone.

"And look how Aunt Amanda turned out. She trapped me in a cell," Max said, shaking Olivia furiously. "A cell!"

"I'm sorry to interrupt, but, Max, you might want to keep it down before your parents wake up," Rick said.

"Olivia? Max?" their mom called from upstairs. "Where are you?"

"We're down here, Mom, with Rick," Olivia said.

"Okay, your father and I will be right down."

"Okay," Olivia said.

"What do you guys usually eat in the morning?" Rick asked, getting up and walking into the kitchen.

"A breakfast buffet if you're going to cook," Max said, following him.

"Max, we never have that, and he probably

doesn't know how to make a breakfast buffet. He hasn't cooked in seven years. We usually have toast. Wait. Do we have bread for making toast?" Olivia said, whacking Max on the back of his head.

"The cooking part is true, but toast I can make. The only problem is, I have no clue if there's bread."

"Good morning, Rick," Olivia's mom said, walking down the stairs. "How did everyone sleep?"

"I don't know. I still think I'd be better in a king-size bed," Max said, placing an imaginary crown on his head.

"You do not need a king-size bed, Max. We slept fine, Mom. Where's Dad?" Olivia asked.

"Your dad is still upstairs getting dressed. Now what do you kids want for breakfast?"

"Well, Mrs. Lockhart, I was going to make breakfast for them, but I don't know if we have any bread," Rick said.

"Oh, that's so nice of you, and yes, we do have bread, but there's no reason for you to make us all breakfast."

"No, it's fine. Really. You guys are letting me stay here. Just think of this as a thank you," Rick said, getting the bread out of the refrigerator and placing it in the toaster.

After breakfast, their mom handed Olivia a flyer about the vendor site outside the hotel on the boardwalk that day.

"Are you sure we should be doing activities already instead of finding out a little bit more about where Aunt Amanda is?" Olivia said.

"Olivia, I know you want to know what happened, but I'm sure the police will catch her. It's too dangerous to go after her. We have no clue what she's up to," Olivia's mom warned.

"Exactly, we have no clue what she's up to, so we should find out. We know more about Aunt Amanda than those cops. Don't you think it would be a good idea for us to investigate for ourselves?" Olivia asked.

"My decision has been made, and it's final." Mom crossed her arms with a stern look on her face.

"Okay, I get it. You are a little scared for us, but we aren't scared. It's time that we all come out of our comfort zone. It's for the best," Olivia stated.

"Olivia, I am not scared myself. I—" her mom began, but she got cut off by Max.

"Okay, I know that Olivia said me and her aren't scared, but she doesn't speak the truth for me," Max said, biting his fingernails.

"See, your brother doesn't want to go either. It's just you, Olivia, and you can't go alone. It's too dangerous, and if I go with you, I'd have to bring Max," Olivia's mom argued.

"So? Max can stay with Dad or Rick. Rick could even come with us, but that's all up to him."

"Sweetie, I don't want to go. Plus, it would be bringing you into trouble, too. And honestly, I do not trust Rick entirely yet," Olivia's mom said, looking over at Rick, who was still sitting at the kitchen table eating breakfast.

"If you don't trust him entirely, then why are you letting him stay here? And you are scared. You just don't want to admit it," Olivia shot back, crossing her arms.

"Olivia, don't you dare talk back to me like that. You are not going, and neither is Max, Rick, me, or your father. We are all staying together and going to the vendor event," Olivia's mom fumed, walking away.

Olivia rushed over to Max and said, "This is perfect. We're going to the vendor event, and remember Aunt Amanda was working at one of the stores at the boardwalk where the vendors are. Bet you anything she's hiding out there."

"You really think that she would go back to a

place where you know she has been. That's just flat out stupidity," Max said.

"That's what she wants people to think, so we wouldn't suspect that's where she's hiding, I bet," Olivia said, getting a jolt of excitement.

"Listen, if you want to capture a villain, you've gotta think like one," Max said.

Rick got up from the kitchen table and headed over to Olivia and Max in the living room. "Let me get this straight. You are going to capture Amanda even though your mom specifically said not to, and Max is helping? I'm with your mother. You can not go without an adult."

"Exactly, so you have to come with us. I did save your life by getting you out of Aunt Amanda's lair and letting you stay here," Olivia said with a mischievous look on her face.

"Technically, your mom let me stay here, so I'm with her for that reason and because it is dangerous. For instance, Amanda trapped me in her underground lair and made me stay there for seven years," Rick said.

"I talked Mom into it, so if it weren't for *me*, you wouldn't be here," Olivia said.

"Okay, I see both of your points, but I'm with

Olivia here. I want to be a hero and fight crime," Max said, putting a fist in the air.

"Max, no. You can't go either. No one is going. We are listening to your mom and staying together and only shopping at the vendors. No going into that store. Do you hear me?" Rick asked.

"When did you turn into one of our parents?" Max asked.

"Olivia! Max! Go get dressed. We're heading down to the vendor event as soon as you're ready," Olivia's dad yelled down to them. Their dad came walking down the stairs already dressed and grabbed a piece of toast off the counter, while Olivia and Max rushed up the stairs to get dressed.

Once Olivia and Max were ready, they went downstairs to meet up with Rick and their parents, who were waiting by the door.

"Are you guys ready now so we can head down to the vendors?" Olivia's mom asked, ruffling Max's hair.

"Yup, I think so," Olivia said.

"All right then. Let's go," their dad said.

Rick opened the door, and they headed toward the elevator to go downstairs. Once they got inside the elevator, Olivia noticed a poster for movie night at the hotel. There was a picture of a dog on it with the same sunglasses she was wearing. Olivia took off her sunglasses and put them next to the picture.

"Olivia, I didn't know you were a model for movie night," Max said, chuckling.

Olivia lightly punched Max on the arm. "That's because I'm not."

Once they were there, the sun coming through the lobby doors immediately blinded them. They opened the door and saw vendors crowding the boardwalks on each side.

"Okay, Olivia, here's ten dollars for you, and Max, here's ten dollars for you. I will be shopping with Max, and your dad will watch Olivia. And Rick..." Olivia's mom paused. "Here's some money for you. You'll probably need to get clothes or something."

"Oh, thank you, but you really don't have to," Rick said.

"No, please, keep it. Use it. I wouldn't be able to use it for as good a cause," Olivia's mom said right before Max snuck away and ran into all the vendors. Olivia's mom quickly chased after him.

"Rick, you can come with us," Olivia said.

"Um, sure. So, where do we start?" Rick asked.

"Rick, can you watch Olivia for a second? It looks like Max isn't behaving for your mother, Olivia. I better go take care of things," Olivia's dad said.

"Sure thing, Mr. Lockhart," Rick said, saluting him. "I won't let her out of my sight. Right, Olivia?" Rick turned around and saw Olivia was no longer behind him. "Olivia?"

Olivia heard Rick calling for her. Obviously, he had noticed she was trying to get away and look for Amanda on her own so Rick would not stop her. Olivia closed her eyes and slid behind one of the shops, hoping Rick wouldn't find her. Suddenly, she saw a girl with red hair through the window, who looked exactly like the girl from the gelato place except for the red hair. Olivia wanted to investigate, so she peeked around the corner to see if Rick was looking in her direction. Fortunately, he was looking in the opposite direction. Then she quickly went around the building and into the shop.

"Excuse me, but do I know you?" Olivia asked, walking up to the girl.

"Um, no. I don't think so," the girl replied.

Olivia saw a brown slither of hair coming out from under the girl's red hair. Olivia's eyes widened. She must have been wearing a wig!

"Yes, I do. You were that girl spying on me and my family at the gelato place last night!" Olivia exclaimed pointing at the girl.

The girl quickly pushed Olivia aside, making her fall, and ran out of the shop.

CHAPTER FIVE

MORE THAN JUST A GNARLY TREE

O livia quickly got up and ran after the girl. She was determined to catch her. When she ran out, Olivia realized Rick saw her run out of the store. "I really should have planned this out," Olivia whispered to herself, still running at full speed.

Soon, she came to a stop and hid behind a gnarly tree when she saw the girl placing her hand on a branch and pulling down, opening a secret door. She stepped inside the tree, and the door closed. Olivia came out from behind the tree and pulled on the branch to make the door open again. Then she jumped in when she saw Rick coming around the corner of the building. The door quickly shut before Rick could see anything happen. Olivia was surrounded by darkness. Then she felt herself lowering as if she were in some sort of elevator. Soon, she stopped lowering and the door opened up to a lair.

"Hello?" Olivia called out. "Is anybody down here?"

No answer.

Olivia stepped out of the elevator and decided to look around. Lanterns were lit up bordering the room. Olivia walked up to a desk and saw a bunch of letters that were signed to Alex from A.W.

"A.W.?" Olivia said to herself. "Amanda Walters! Well, how would this girl know Amanda? Or is it a different person with the initials A.W.? Maybe she knows where Aunt Amanda is."

"You shouldn't be down here," a voice yelled. The girl stepped out from a long hallway, bringing herself into the light. "Who are you? And why are you here?"

"My name is Olivia Lockhart, and you were the one spying on me and my family at the gelato place. Remember, I talked to you at the store? I followed you here. I want answers," Olivia explained.

"You wouldn't understand," the girl said. "You don't know what I've been through!"

"Trust me, after what has happened the past few days, I am pretty sure your situation could not be worse than mine," Olivia fumed, pointing at the girl. "Now tell me why you were spying on me!"

"I saw you going into the forest. I wanted to warn you, but once you entered through the waterfall, I didn't think there was much chance. So, when you came out, I wanted to see if you were all right and what happened. But you seem fine, so it looks like I don't need to worry about you and you don't need to worry about me."

"Oh. Sorry, I kind of went all up at you right there, then. I didn't know," Olivia apologized.

"It's fine. I'm Alex, by the way. Honestly, I would have done the same if I was in your position," Alex said.

"There's just one thing before we carry on talking. Those letters over there... Um, who's the person who sent those?" Olivia asked, looking back over at the letters on the desk.

"Why do you want to know? That's my personal business."

"Well, I was just curious and—"

"Listen, I would never ask who sent letters to you. Personal business is personal business, and I don't even know you at all," Alex pointed out.

The elevator door opened, and Rick stepped out from inside it.

"Rick?" Olivia asked. "How did you find me down here?"

"I saw you get into the tree, and then a tree branch moved up. I tried pulling it down, and the door opened," Rick explained. "Who's that?"

"I'm Alex, the one she followed down here."

"Olivia, why would you follow her?" Rick asked. "You don't even know her."

"Exactly," Alex said.

"She was the girl I saw spying on us last night. Remember I told you?" Olivia didn't have time to answer Rick's questions. She wanted time for Alex to answer all of *her* questions.

"Well, yeah I remember that, but... Wait a second. How do you have an underground lair in a gnarly tree?" Rick asked, finally taking a good look at the lair.

"Well, I never really had a home, so I kind of just built this place. I went into the dumps, picked up all the stuff, and made it all work again," Alex said.

"What about your parents? Don't you have any?" Olivia asked.

"Well, yes, but they kind of died when I was a baby. So I just had to keep in contact with my aunt, but she lives in New York and I'm too young to fly on a plane alone. That's who sent me the letters."

"So that's your answer?" Rick asked.

"Um, yeah. I even have proof." Alex walked over and took a picture off an old bulletin board. She handed it to Rick. "That's my aunt."

"Yeah, that's pretty believable," Rick said, handing the picture back to Alex. "Sorry to leave you here, but Olivia, we have to go."

"Rick, she has no home. We can't just leave her here."

"It's nice of you to take me in, but don't you think it would be a little bit much to take Alex in?" Rick asked, gesturing to Alex.

"Rick, she's my age, and I've always wanted a sister. I don't have any cousins to keep in contact with. And plus, she's way too young to stay here alone."

"I'll let you two work this out, but she can not come. I'm going back up. You come up when you're done," Rick said.

"Fine. I'll be right up," Olivia said as Rick stepped into the elevator.

"So, what was inside that waterfall?" Alex asked.

"Well, there was this crazy lady who I didn't know was a family member but turned out to be, and she's kind of evil. She got away, and I want to find her."

"What did she look like?" Alex asked.

"Well, I'm not really sure if she was in a costume again or not, because she kind of lured me here and trapped my family and...yeah," Olivia explained.

"It's weird because my aunt has a sister just like that. She's evil, and she tried to kidnap me. So we basically lost track of where she is. Her name is Amanda Walters, and my aunt's name is Ashley Walters."

"Wait a second! Amanda Walters? That's her! She's my aunt. And wait! Did you say Ashley Walters? So my mom has another secret sister?" Olivia asked in disbelief with her hands palms up in the air.

"Actually two because of my mom, who died in a car crash."

"What? But how did my mom never tell me about them? How many secrets is she keeping?" Olivia couldn't believe she had three aunts she never knew about until she was twelve.

"That means we are cousins!" Alex exclaimed.

"That's awesome! Now Rick and my parents have to let you stay. If you're family, you automatically have to come home with us."

"Well, since we're family, I probably should tell you the truth." Alex paused before finally deciding to tell Olivia. "I know where Amanda is."

CHAPTER SIX

AMARA WETLANDS

"What? You know where Amanda is?" Olivia asked, feeling like everything had just changed right in front of her eyes.

"Yes. Here." Alex handed Olivia two plane tickets to Amara Wetlands.

"Where is Amara Wetlands?" Olivia asked, reading the name off the tickets.

"Where Amanda is," Alex explained. "I've been trying to track her down ever since I found out she was evil. I got the tickets, hoping to go there. If I got two tickets, it was cheaper because of the deal, but I figure you would want to come and try to help since you've been trying to capture her, too."

"But I could never run away without my family—especially not without Max. It was too dangerous the first time."

"Who's Max?" Alex asked.

"He's my annoying little brother."

"Then why do you want to bring him?" Alex asked.

"He's family. Plus, he'd probably steal all my stuff while I was gone," Olivia explained.

"Yeah, that makes sense," Alex said. "Do you need to bring anyone else?"

"Is there any chance I could bring Rick?" Olivia asked.

"I don't have enough money to pay for everyone. And wasn't he the guy who was going to leave me here in the first place?"

"He could be helpful, though. He was Amanda's prisoner for seven years," Olivia explained.

"What about your parents? Wouldn't you want them to come, too?"

"They don't want me going after Amanda. They say it's too dangerous."

"It is dangerous, but it's better than doing nothing about it. Also, since we're family, I guess I should tell you that my mother didn't die in a car crash. It was all Amanda's fault. Amanda wanted my mom to join her in being evil, but she said no, so Amanda got back at her by killing her."

"I could never live my life without my mom. My mom would definitely say yes to coming if you told her that."

"Then come on. We'll all go, but I can't afford the tickets. Your parents would have to buy more."

"I'm sure they would love to if it meant getting to capture Amanda and helping their niece," Olivia said.

"Great. Let's go and tell them the news," Alex said.

"Don't you want to pack anything first?"

"What would I need to pack? I barely have anything. I only have the essentials."

"All right. Come on. The sooner, the better," Olivia said.

They stepped into the elevator to meet Rick at the top.

"*She's* here? I told you she can not come," Rick fumed.

"Rick, she's my cousin," Olivia explained.

"Your what? Oh, come on. Anyone can say that. How can you trust her? She's just a random girl you found spying on you."

"My aunt is Amanda, who killed my mom, Sadie. And I know where Amanda is. We are going to try to capture her," Alex explained.

"Wow. It was almost as if you just planned that out," Rick said. "Or did you? Are you working for Amanda?"

"She killed my mom!" Alex said with tears in her eyes.

Olivia put her arm around Alex to try to calm her down. "Let's go meet up with Max and my parents," Olivia said.

They headed over to find that Max was climbing a

palm tree while Olivia's mom and dad were trying to get him down.

"At least your brother isn't like that guy trying to climb the palm tree over there. Then I'd understand why you said he was annoying," Alex said.

Olivia looked at Alex and didn't say anything.

"Oh wait. Is that your brother?" Alex asked, realizing it probably could be.

"Yes. Yes, it is," Olivia said, shaking her head in disappointment.

"I feel so bad. How do you live with him?"

"I honestly don't know anymore."

"Who's that?" Max asked, jumping down from the opposite side of the tree his parents' where guarding. He ran over to Olivia and Rick.

"Max, this is Alex, our cousin," Olivia said, gesturing toward Alex.

Max burst out laughing and said, "We don't have a cousin. Don't tell me you've been fooled by someone else."

"Max, I'm not kidding. I'll explain it to you once we have Mom and Dad's attention because Mom was hiding something from us *again*," Olivia explained.

"Again? How many things can one person possibly hide?" Max said as their parents finally caught up.

"Olivia, Rick, where have you been?" Olivia's dad asked. "You disappeared when I was trying to get Max down from the tree. I was going to go after you, but here you are."

"I saw a girl in the store and chased after her into a gnarly tree, and Olivia got worried and chased after me and—" Rick started to say, but he got cut off by Olivia.

"Rick, they should know the truth. I've lied enough," Olivia said. "The truth is, last night when we were at the gelato place, I saw a girl spying on us. And then I went in a store because I thought I saw the girl again, and it turned out to be her," she said, gesturing to Alex. "I followed her into a gnarly tree, which was her home because her mom, Sadie, died because of Aunt Amanda and you never even told me that I had a cousin or another aunt and that Alex has an aunt named Ashley, which means you had three sisters that you never told us about. How long did you think you could keep this up?" Olivia's face turned as red as her shirt after blurting that all out.

"Cousin? Sadie never had a daughter," Olivia's mom said.

"There are two more?" Olivia's father cut in.

"So you admit there's a Sadie?" Olivia asked.

"Yes, but Sadie never had a daughter that I knew

about," Olivia's mom said, staring at Alex with a confused look on her face.

"You see my mom had me after she moved out. I was only four when she died. I've lived alone in that gnarly tree for the past nine years. You never found out about me because you never kept in contact with my mom," Alex explained.

"Wait a second. What's your name?" Olivia's mom asked.

"My name is Alex."

"Three sisters?" Olivia's dad asked again.

"Yes, three sisters," Olivia's mom said.

"Wait a second. How come we never knew about the other sisters?" Olivia asked.

"Well, if I told you about Sadie, then you would probably ask me where she is, and I didn't want you finding out about Amanda because she was nothing but trouble. Ashley disappeared one night when we were little. We don't know what happened to her. Back at the gelato place, I tried searching online for Ashley or where she might be, thinking Amanda might have gone to her, but I couldn't find anything."

"I might know where she is," Alex said. Alex showed Olivia's mom the tickets to Amara Wetlands.

"How is this going to help us?" Olivia's mom asked.

"It's where Amanda is. I've been tracking her down," Alex said. "You'd need to buy more tickets, though. I only have two tickets. I was going to bring Olivia, but she wanted to bring you and Max and her dad and Rick."

"Well, I'd have to tell your grandparents, but if you might know where Ashley is too, then I'll go," Olivia's mom said.

Alex turned to Olivia. "You don't want to bring your grandparents too, do you? Or are you good?"

"Okay, listen," Olivia's dad said. "My parents are not coming. I don't want them getting involved in all this. I'm not sure *I* want to be involved in all this."

"We have three children to look after. With all the mischief that's been going on with these children, we should at least have one adult with one child," Olivia's mom said.

"Do I have to go?" Olivia's dad whined, sounding a lot like Max.

Olivia and her mom crossed their arms and stared at Olivia's Dad.

"Fine," Olivia's dad said, crossing his arms and walking over to the side of the building with Max following.

"We should go get the tickets right now before it's

too late. We need to start immediately," Olivia's mom suggested.

"Three sisters? Can you believe it?" Olivia's dad asked Max.

"I know, right? How can it be possible?" Max replied.

"Would you two quit messing around and help us get the tickets?"

There was nothing that was going to get in Olivia's way of catching Aunt Amanda and getting her invention notebook back.

CHAPTER SEVEN
FAMILY SECRETS

Back at the hotel, everyone was packing their stuff.

"So, this is where you live?" Alex asked, picking up a conk shell on the table.

"Actually, we live in New Jersey. This was supposed to be a vacation with our grandparents, believe it or not," Olivia explained.

Alex put the shell down and looked at Olivia with a sorry and confused expression on her face. "Seriously? I feel so bad now. You and your family should have some fun while you are here. I'll go by myself."

"Are you crazy? I am not going to stay here and do nothing when you are trying to catch Amanda," Olivia said, putting her hand on Alex's shoulder. "You could get hurt. Plus, we are family. That's not how family works."

"Are you sure? I mean that's sweet of you and all, but I'm serious. This place is amazing. I can't let you miss out on all the great stuff here just because of me," Alex said, taking Olivia's hand off her shoulder.

"And I can't let you go alone," Olivia said.

"Okay, does everyone have what they need so we can get going?" Olivia's mom asked, bringing her bag downstairs with Olivia's dad close behind.

"More like get this over with," Olivia's dad mumbled.

"Other than Max and Dad, yes," Olivia answered.

"What?" Dad replied. "I'm packed."

"I can hear it when you mumble, you know," Olivia said.

"Max, hurry up!" Olivia's mom called.

"Fine," Max said, walking down the stairs.

"Where are your bags?" Olivia asked.

"Upstairs," Max answered, gesturing up the stairs. "Rick, be a good man and go fetch them for me," Max said, waving his hand in the air.

"Max!" Olivia scolded him. "Go get it yourself."

"Oh, come on. If he can work for Aunt Amanda, he can work for me. I mean, who's worse? I never killed anyone." Max turned to Alex. "What? Too soon?"

"You're lucky he's your brother," Alex said, turning to Olivia.

"Max, cut it out and go get your stuff."

"Fine," Max said, crossing his arms and stomping up the steps.

"I'm so sorry about him, Rick," Olivia's mom said.

"Yeah, he can be a real pain. Believe me," Olivia said, rolling her eyes.

Soon, Max was coming down the stairs. "I heard all that," Max said, glaring at Olivia. "Here, Rick," Max said, tossing the bag into Rick's arms. "Be a gentleman and carry them the whole way there, would you? Oh, and if you have time—"

"Max!" Olivia's mom said. "How about you be a gentleman and carry Rick's bag?"

"He has one of those things? Where was he keeping it for the past seven years?" Max asked.

"Your parents gave me money to buy a bag and some clothes, remember?" Rick said. "But you don't have to carry my bag."

"I'm not going to argue with that," Max said. "You're still carrying my bag, though, right?"

"No, he is not!" Olivia said.

"Um, don't you think we should get out of here soon to get the rest of the tickets before the plane takes off?" Alex asked.

"When does the plane take off?" Olivia's dad asked.

"Noon, so we still have enough time to eat a small lunch, get the tickets, and go through security if we leave now," Alex said.

"All right, everybody. Come on," Olivia's mom said. "Out the door we go."

When they got to the lobby, the woman at the

front desk asked, "Where are you off to this morning?"

"Um, places," Max said.

"What places?" the woman said. "Because I highly recommend that you go to the vendors at night. They swarm over by Señor Frog's and JH Yee's. But during the daytime, the only ones you'll find around here are the ones that always come around on Thursdays."

"We've already checked the vendors this morning, but we'll try to check them this evening," Olivia's mom lied.

"Well, enjoy your day," the woman said.

When they got outside, they flagged down a taxi to take them to the airport.

"Leaving already? The last plane came in just a couple of days ago," the taxi driver said. "Unless you didn't take that flight."

"Um, we actually came here on a different day," Olivia's dad lied.

"Normally I don't see such small bags for so many people. There aren't even enough bags for all of you," the driver said, opening the taxi door.

"Thank you," Olivia's mom said, stepping inside and ignoring his comment.

Once they were at the airport, Olivia's mom said, "I'll get the tickets, and you kids wait over by the food court, okay? Rick, would you mind staying with the children?"

"Not at all, Mrs. Lockhart," Rick said, saluting her.

Olivia's parents walked away to go get the tickets.

"So, Alex, how long is the flight?" Olivia asked, looking at her watch.

"It's about two and a half or three hours," Alex said.

"If I were in a position like Amanda, I would not go somewhere that is almost three hours away," Max said.

Olivia's parents were already on their way back by the time Max had finished talking.

"How are you guys back already?" Olivia asked.

"There was no one on line to get tickets," her mom answered. "And they were surprisingly cheap."

"Not that surprising," Alex said.

"Why?" Olivia asked. "Amara Wetlands sounds like a beautiful place."

"It used to be," Alex said. "I'll tell you more about it on the plane ride."

"All right, did you kids scout out where you want to have a quick lunch before we take off?" Olivia's dad asked.

"How about the hot pretzel stand?" Max said. "It will fit into Rick's budget."

"Max, give the man a break!" Olivia's mom scolded.

"Fine, fine. Olivia will pay."

"Um, no way I'm paying. I'll pay for my own but not yours."

"Your dad is paying, so quit arguing," Olivia's mom said.

"I am?" Olivia's dad asked.

Olivia's mom turned and glared at her husband.

"I mean, I am," Olivia's dad said. "How much are they?"

"Six dollars each," Rick said. "There's a sign over there."

"Six dollars? Oh, come on? Couldn't Max pay?" Olivia's dad whined.

"How did I get involved in this?" Max complained.

"Both of you behave!" Olivia's mom said.

After they ate their pretzels, the flight was ready to board. Olivia was excited to finally have Alex all to herself to ask more questions about the family secrets since she obviously wasn't going to get any more out of her mom. Who knew what else she was hiding?

CHAPTER EIGHT
THE LOST ISLAND

W hen they boarded the plane, Olivia noticed there was no line. She and Alex found their seats near the front of the plane. The rest of the family and Rick kept walking a few rows back. Olivia wondered why their seats were separated since there weren't any other people on the plane except a blonde woman wearing a pink fedora sitting in the row across from Max.

"Um, excuse me, ma'am. Is there a reason no one is on the plane except us?" Olivia's mom asked the woman.

"Well, it's not exactly the place people would want to vacation at," the lady replied. "Are you here vacationing with your son and husband?"

"Um, actually, I have a daughter and niece here, too," Olivia's mom said, gesturing toward Olivia and Alex, who were four rows in front of them.

"Hopefully the place has improved over time," the woman said, turning away and getting a book out of her bag. It almost seemed like the woman was trying to avoid talking to Olivia's mom.

"So tell me about the island," Olivia said, turning toward Alex and away from the conversation between her mom and the woman. She clicked her seat belt as the stewardess came around to make sure everyone was ready to take off.

"Well, it was beautiful. Everyone was crowding the flights. You could rarely even get a seat," Alex explained, looking around at the empty cabin. "You see, when I was little, I used to go snorkeling there with my mom. We would stay for a week every four months or so. We loved it there and wouldn't have changed a single thing about the island." Alex's voice trembled as if she was holding back tears.

"What do you mean *was* beautiful?" Olivia asked, not even noticing that the plane was taking off.

"You see, Amanda wanted to rule that place. Wipe all the smiles off people's faces, and she got her wish. She rules there right now. Everyone on the island has never come off since she took over. The rumor spread, and no one has wanted to go there since. All you hear are screams and cries for help—not laughter. The people used to hang lanterns and have parties in the caves, but now no one comes out with all their limbs."

Olivia's eyes widened in horror.

"Okay, I might have exaggerated a little on that last one," Alex said. "No one dares to go in the caves anymore."

"You better be exaggerating," Olivia replied, suddenly nervous to be going to Amara Wetlands.

"The island has changed so much people call it The Lost Island," Alex explained.

Olivia turned in her seat to look at the lady on the flight with them. "Why do you think this woman is on the plane if it's such a terrible place?" Olivia asked, confused why anyone else would go to such a scary place.

"I'm not sure. Normally, there is no one on the plane anymore," Alex said, looking back at the woman like she was crazy. "She kind of looks familiar to me. She reminds me a little bit of how Ashley looks."

"Maybe she *is* Ashley!" Olivia exclaimed, checking to see if the seat belt symbol was light up or not. Noticing it wasn't, she got up and went over to her mom. "Hey, Mom, does she look like Ashley to you?" Olivia asked, gesturing to the woman.

"Hold on," Olivia's mom said. "I'm not sure. Let me see." She turned toward the woman. "Excuse me, but do I know you?"

"I don't think so." The woman shook her head.

"What's your name?" Olivia asked her.

"Ashley," the woman replied. "Why?"

"Ashley Walters?" Olivia's mom asked, raising her hand to her mouth in disbelief.

"Yes. How did you know?" Ashley asked with a surprised look on her face.

"I'm Sara Brooks, your half sister," Olivia's mom replied.

CHAPTER NINE
UNWANTED REUNION

"I can't believe this. I'm finally meeting you again after all these years," Ashley said.

"Whatever happened to you when you disappeared? Where did you go?" Olivia's mom asked.

"I had a feeling that we'd find you if we went to Amara Wetlands," Alex interrupted. "Knowing you, you'd also try to stop Amanda."

"Who are you?" Ashley asked.

"Your niece, Alex. The one you've been writing to," Alex said.

"Oh, Alexandra, you must be scared living all by yourself in Abura," Ashley said.

"Whoa, whoa, whoa. Wait a second. Alexandra?" Max asked.

"Um, Max, Alex is short for Alexandra," Olivia pointed out. "She just likes to be called Alex."

"Yeah, *Alexandra* kind of makes me sound weak for some reason," Alex said.

"So you want to sound tough like me, huh?" Max asked.

"Not even close," Alex said. "Is that what I seem like to you?" she asked Olivia, sounding a little worried.

"Trust me; if you were anything like him, I would have left you in that gnarly tree," Olivia said.

"Okay, wait a second. Why is Ashley here?" Max asked, turning around to look at Ashley.

"Um, I'll answer that once I use the restroom," Ashley said, grabbing her backpack and walking toward the bathroom at the front of the plane.

"Who brings a backpack to go use the bathroom?" Olivia asked.

"Maybe she brought her own soap and toilet paper," Max said. "Or a newspaper to read," he added with a shrug.

Everyone looked at Max in silent disbelief.

"What?" he asked. "It could happen."

"We'll find out if she comes back, because right now I'm not trusting her so much," Alex said, looking toward the front of the plane.

Once everyone was back in their seats, Olivia realized ten minutes had passed and there was still no sign of Ashley. "Shouldn't Ashley have been back by now?" Olivia asked Alex.

"Maybe nature called," Max said.

"Were you eavesdropping?" Olivia asked.

"Ew, that would be disgusting!" Max said.

"Not on Ashley! On Alex and me," Olivia said.

Soon the plane landed, and there was still no sign of Ashley.

"All right, Olivia and Max, get your bags. You too, Alex," Olivia's mom said. "We have to get off the plane."

"But what about Ashley?" Olivia asked.

"It must have been a big one," Max said. "I hope she didn't fall in when the plane landed."

"Max, I'm positive she didn't fall in the toilet," Olivia said.

"How do you know? We never saw her come out of the bathroom," Max said.

"We should probably get going by now," Alex said. "We've wasted enough time here, and Ashley obviously does not want to be around us."

"Alex is right. Come on everyone," Olivia's dad said, getting out of his seat.

When they went to get off the plane, Olivia noticed that the bathroom was no longer occupied. Then she saw blonde hair disappear around the corner. "Um, guys. I think Ashley just got off the plane."

"It doesn't matter," Alex said. "She's not going to be any help to us."

"She might be," Olivia said. "What if she came here because of Amanda, too?"

"There is a possibility, but how will we find out?" Alex asked.

"We follow her," Olivia said, hoping one of her secret aunts would lead her to another.

CHAPTER TEN
FOLLOW THE LEADER

Once they got off the plane, Olivia said, "Guys, look. Ashley is over there. Come on."

Alex followed Olivia toward Ashley. "Wait. Are you sure this is a good idea, just following her? Who knows where she could be taking us?"

"Okay, calm down. First of all, she doesn't even know that we're following her. Second of all, where else would she be going? I doubt she'd want to be trapped here, especially after everything has changed like this," Olivia said, pulling Alex toward the door.

"Okay, fine," Alex said. "We'll follow her. Come on, guys."

"Welcome to The Lost Island," a worker groaned as they walked past.

They walked out the door and saw Ashley in the car rental parking lot, getting into a car.

"Great. How are we going to catch up to her now if she has a car and we don't?" Olivia asked.

"We take one," Alex said.

"Whoa, whoa, whoa. We are not stealing any cars. I didn't want to come here in the first place, and the last thing I want to do is steal a car from an airport," Olivia's dad said.

"Oh, come on, Dad," Olivia said.

"Cool! We're stealing a car!" Max said.

"Max, keep it down," Olivia said.

"We are not stealing a car," Olivia's dad said.

Olivia's mom looked at him. "Ashley could be in danger if she goes to find Amanda on her own. I would never want that to happen to my sister. We'll return the car later."

Olivia's dad shook his head. "No, no, no. No way am I driving a car that was stolen."

"Fine, you don't have to. I will," Olivia's mom said.

They headed over to an SUV.

"How are we all going to fit in this thing?" Max asked.

"I will drive. Your dad will sit in the passenger seat. Rick, Olivia, and Alex will sit in the back seat, and you... What exactly are we going to do with you?" Olivia's mom asked.

"Trunk?" Olivia suggested. "Hey, come on. It's our best bet."

"All right, Max. In the trunk," Olivia's mom said.

"Cool, no seat belt," Max said.

"Wait a second. How are we getting in this car?" Olivia asked.

"Easy," Alex said. "I can hack into the keypad on the driver's door and unlock the car."

"While you do that, everyone give me their bags so that way once she pops the trunk I can put it all in with Max."

"I'm going to be squished in a trunk by bags?" Max asked.

"Yeah, pretty much," Olivia said.

"Um, guys. Ashley just pulled out of the parking lot," Rick said.

"Don't worry," Alex said, typing on the keypad. "I got it unlocked. And look, the key is in the middle console!"

"All right, everybody, in the car," Olivia's mom said.

Once they were on the dirt road, they started seeing dying flowers and trees, caves, bears, lots of forests, and very little sunlight through all the gray clouds.

"I know you said this place was gloomy, but I didn't think you meant *this* gloomy," Olivia said.

Soon, Ashley's car stopped and pulled over. She got out and headed toward a huge cave.

"What is she doing?" Olivia said as her mom pulled the SUV over to the side of the road, keeping some distance between them and Ashley's vehicle.

"Whatever she's doing is in that cave," Alex said as Ashley disappeared into the shadows of the cave.

"Oh darn, I guess she got away," Max said, cowering behind the back seat.

"Max, we're going to follow her," Olivia said, staring into the dark cave, not mentioning that she was scared herself.

CHAPTER ELEVEN
TRAPPED

They got out of the car and let Max out of the trunk.

"Max?" Olivia's dad asked.

"Max isn't here right now. Leave a message at the tone," Max mumbled from underneath the backpacks. "*Beeeeeeep.*"

"Oh, come on, Max. There's nothing to be afraid of," Rick said.

"Oh, this is just ridiculous," Alex said, starting to pull the backpacks off of Max.

"I am not scared," Max said.

"If you aren't scared, then get out of the trunk," Olivia said.

"Why do you have to be so wise?" Max asked.

"I don't have time for this," Alex said, starting off toward the cave.

Olivia quickly got her backpack on and followed Alex, pulling Max behind her. Max tried to hang on to his backpack in the trunk to keep from going into the cave, but it just ended up coming with him.

"Everyone, wait up. We have to stick together," Olivia's mom said.

Olivia saw that Alex didn't stop when her mom told her to. Olivia turned around and looked at her mom. Then she turned to Alex and kept walking.

"Alex, wait up. Listen, I know you want to get in there and see where Ashley is going, but we have to stick together like my mom said."

"If we stick together, then we'll probably be slowed down by one another, and I want to get there as quickly as possible. I'm not waiting for anybody," Alex said.

"Alex, you still have to follow what my mom says. You're just a kid."

"*Just* a kid? I grew up in that gnarly tree all alone. I think I can handle going through a cave alone," Alex said, speeding up.

"Alex, you are not going alone. We have to stick together," Olivia said, reaching for Alex's backpack, but Alex pulled away.

They walked through the entrance of the cave.

"Is there a possibility anyone brought a flash-light?" Max asked.

"I guess I could use my phone," Olivia said, getting her phone out of her backpack.

"And I have a flashlight in my backpack," Olivia's dad said, already getting it out of his bag.

"Um, can I use that?" Alex asked, pointing at the flashlight.

"First they drag me to this island, and then I can't

even use my own flashlight?" Olivia's dad said, handing it to Alex.

"Oh, cut it out, you big baby. Just use the flashlight on your phone," Olivia's mom said.

Pieces of the cave ceiling started falling to the ground, the sounds echoing throughout the cave. They tried to get away from the falling rock by rushing further into the cave. Bigger chunks of rock started to fall from the ceiling, blocking the entrance.

"Why couldn't I just be back in the trunk?" Max mumbled to himself.

"Is everyone okay?" Olivia's mom asked.

"Yes, we're all fine, Mom," Olivia said. "But we should probably get away from the entrance in case more rocks fall."

"Or we could use Rick as a human shield and just get out of this cave," Max suggested.

Boom!

The whole entrance to the cave collapsed, showing no way out.

Max jumped into Olivia's arms.

"Don't worry, everyone. It's going to be okay," Olivia's mom said. "Hopefully," she mumbled under her breath.

"We're all going to die!" Max said.

"No, we won't, Max," Olivia said, dropping him to the ground. "We'll find another way out." She looked toward the other side of the cave. "I think I see a little bit of sunlight over there," Olivia said, pointing further into the cave. "Maybe that's the way out."

"Impossible," Alex said. "No cave on this island would ever be that short. And plus there's more darkness after that, so I doubt it's a way out."

"Hopefully you're wrong," Olivia said, starting to walk through the cave. She used her flashlight on her phone to look around. She saw bats sleeping upside down. It started getting colder and colder as they walked deeper into the cave.

"How big is this place?" Max asked. "We've been walking for hours."

"Um, we really haven't," Olivia said. She looked back to see Max wasn't even walking. Her dad was carrying him.

"What?" Max asked. "Rick wouldn't do it and my feet were hurting."

"How? We've only been in this cave for like five minutes," Olivia said.

"And I've been carrying you for three of those minutes," Olivia's dad said.

Alex rolled her eyes and kept walking.

"All right, everyone. Focus," Olivia said. "We aren't going to get anywhere by—"

"Olivia, look. I see Ashley over there," Alex interrupted, pointing up ahead to Ashley, who had a flashlight in her hand. "I'm going to go after her."

"Alex, no. Wait!" Olivia said, chasing after Alex, but a boulder fell from the top of the cave, blocking Olivia's path. "Well, now what are we going to do? Alex could get hurt. She's out there by herself."

CHAPTER TWELVE

NEVER ASK A PIRATE FOR A FAVOR

"There has to be some way to get on the other side of the rock," Olivia said, starting to look around.

"As much as I'd like to believe that, I doubt it's true," Max said.

"Hey, Mom, look at this. It looks like Aunt Amanda's business symbol," Olivia said, squatting down and pointing to a piece of slate with the symbol for Aunt Amanda's company, Original Artistry.

"I'm starting to think maybe she really is a Death Eater," Max said. "Why else would her company's symbol look like the Deathly Hollows?"

"Max, it's an O and an A for Original Artistry, and it just happens to be inside a triangle," Olivia said.

"Fine. Whatever," Max said, pushing Olivia and making her step on the piece of slate.

Slowly the rock began to rise to reveal a bridge leading across to another part of the cave.

Olivia's eyes widened in disbelief. She was mostly shocked that technically *Max* found a way around the boulder. "Come on. Let's go. We have to find Alex," Olivia said, stepping onto the bridge. She suddenly froze, looking down to find that underneath the bridge, she couldn't see the ground. It was just pitch-black. On either side of her was an opening.

Max walked up to Olivia, who was already halfway down the bridge. They both looked out at a bunch of plants with sunlight beaming down.

"Why couldn't the way we're going lead to that?" Max asked.

"Max, there's no way to get there. The bridge only leads to the other part of the cave. Now come on," Olivia said, tugging on Max's backpack while her parents and Rick followed.

They got to the other side of the bridge, but Olivia's flashlight on her phone flickered off and on and suddenly turned off completely.

"My phone's dead. Now what are we going to do?" Olivia asked.

"Relax. Your dad and I will use our phones," her mother said.

"Maybe only one of you should so that way we don't use up both batteries at once," Olivia said.

Her mom gave her phone to Olivia. Olivia turned to one side of the cave. Her flashlight beamed on a group of tall, dirty people standing in a huddle around what seemed like a map of some sort. Most of them had long hair and smelled like they hadn't showered in years. Olivia froze and put her hand out so Max would hopefully not see the people as well.

"What is—?" Max said, getting cut off as Olivia put her hand over his mouth.

Olivia turned off the flashlight. "Um, maybe we should go the other way," she whispered.

"But what—?" Max said, getting cut off again by Olivia.

"Just listen to what I say," Olivia whispered.

"Um, Olivia," Max said.

"What, Max? What could possibly be so important you have to tell me right now?" Olivia whispered loudly.

"Look behind you," Max said.

Olivia turned around to see a tall man standing behind her.

Olivia's mom pulled Max and Olivia closer to her.

"You aren't supposed to be here!" the man said.

"Sorry. We didn't mean to bother you," Rick said, stepping in front of everyone else. "We were just looking for someone."

"I can guarantee you that whoever you're looking for is not here," the man said. "Now get out!"

"We don't mean to disturb you, but who are you, and why are you here alone?" Rick asked.

"I am not here alone," the man said as the others came up and stood behind him. "And why do you need to know?" he asked.

"We are looking for two people, and not to be rude or anything, but we know you saw two people come through here," Rick said.

"Maybe we did. Maybe we didn't," he said. "A pirate would never say," he said with a smirk.

"Pirate?" Olivia said, trembling with horror.

CHAPTER THIRTEEN

A DEAL IS A DEAL

"Yeah, we're pirates. Why are you so shocked?" one of the girl pirates asked.

"Well, I kind of thought all pirates were pretty much dead by now," Olivia said.

"Well, you'd be wrong. We are pirates that have survived and have not been found—until you came along."

"Um, as much as we would love to hear more, really we need to know where my cousin and aunt are," Olivia said.

"Listen, kid, we'll only tell you what you want to know if you promise not to tell anyone we're here," another pirate said.

"Don't worry. We'll keep your secret. Just tell us where my cousin and aunt are," Olivia said.

The girl pirate pushed the boy pirate aside and said, "I am Braelynn, and this is my brother, Zane. I'm the captain, and this is my crew. So you want to know where your family members went?"

"Yes. I'm Olivia, and this is my little brother, Max. We came here in search of one of our aunts, who is evil."

"The only person who is evil here is our leader Amanda," Braelynn said.

"Yup, that would be her," Olivia said.

"So, why would you want to be chasing a crazy, evil lady?" Braelynn asked.

"Because we need to turn her in to the cops, and plus, she was the one who killed one of my other aunts," Olivia explained. "Do you know where on this island she stays?"

"I'll answer one of your questions at a time, and the first thing I'm going to answer is where your family members went."

"Hold on, a *girl* captain?" Max asked. "But everyone knows men are much stronger than girls," Max said, flexing.

Braelynn started taking out her sword from its holster on her hip.

"I mean, there are always exceptions," Max said, backing away and putting his hands in the air.

"They both went that way," Braelynn said, pointing her sword toward the end of the cave. "I'm assuming that your cousin was following the aunt."

"Yes. You see my aunt doesn't know we're following her, and we're trying to see what she's up to."

"Very well, then. Follow me," Braelynn said, waving them on.

"Mmmmm!"

"What was that?" Olivia asked.

"Um, nothing," Zane said.

"Mmmmmmm!"

"Okay, that was not nothing," Olivia said, looking around the cave.

All of a sudden, a cage fell from the ceiling of the cave. Olivia and the others jumped back, startled. Inside the cage was Alex with her hands tied behind her back and a rope around her mouth as a gag so she couldn't speak.

"Alex!" Olivia exclaimed.

"Stand back," Zane said, taking his sword out in unison with the other pirates.

"Mmmmm! Mmmmmmm!"

"Let her out," Olivia said.

"Olivia, come here right now," her mom said.

Olivia picked up a nearby board and used it to defend herself. Zane took his sword and chopped the board in half.

"Okay, maybe that wasn't such a good idea," Olivia said, throwing the board to the side. Then she noticed a piece of the cage that had broken off when it fell. The piece looked as sharp as a blade. Olivia picked it up and held it out in front of her. "If you let her go, I won't tell anyone you're here," Olivia said.

Braelynn looked at her crew. "Listen, you can't

blackmail us like that. We're the only ones who know where both your aunts are."

"Wait. You know where Amanda is?" Olivia said.

"Plegh. That rope tastes disgusting," Alex said as the rope around her mouth came undone.

"Alex, are you okay?" Olivia asked.

"Yes, I am fine. And by the way, for pirates who have been here for so long, you should really know how to tie a rope better than that," Alex said.

"It doesn't matter because you're never getting out of that cage," Braelynn said. "None of you are getting out of here alive."

CHAPTER FOURTEEN

FROM BAD TO WORSE

"There has to be a way for us to both get what we want," Olivia said.

"So a trade?" Braelynn asked.

Olivia paused for a second, thinking about what a group of pirates would want from her. All she had on her was stuff she'd grabbed from Aunt Amanda's lab —the fake invention notebook, some potions, and inventions of Olivia's that Aunt Amanda had made.

"I have some gum," Max said, spitting some out into his hand. "Do you like winter green flavor?"

"Hard pass," Braelynn said sarcastically. "You're going to have to try harder than that."

"Fine, I surrender," Max said, dumping his backpack. "Here, take this used Band-aid, some dirty socks, and dirty underwear. How about—?" Max said.

"Max, put everything back in your backpack. No one is going to want your dirty underwear or anything else," Olivia said. "And speaking of, why do you even have dirty underwear in your backpack?"

"It was scary in the trunk. I had to change into the clean ones I brought," Max said, his cheeks turning red.

Braelynn took a step back and gave Max a disgusted look.

"How about some money? I have five hundred dollars," Olivia's mom said.

Braelynn took the money from Olivia's mom's hand. "You're getting there, but keep offering."

"No way. I'm only offering one thing," Olivia's mom said. "You've got the money. Now let Alex go."

"Are you saying she's not worth more than five hundred dollars?" Braelynn asked.

"No, it's just that there has to be something else you want," Olivia's mom said.

"Okay, I was thinking about getting a new member for my crew," Braelynn said with a smirk. "How about him?" she asked, pointing to Rick.

Everyone looked at Rick.

"Don't do it," Alex said. "Go on without me. I'll be fine."

"No, I'll do it," Rick said. "As long as I know that you'll defeat Amanda, that's all that matters. That's what I'm here to do," Rick said, handing himself over to the pirates.

"Rick, no!" Alex said.

"Catch Amanda. You don't need me for that," Rick said.

"So is it a deal, or do I get to keep the kid?" Braelynn asked.

"It's a deal," Rick said.

As soon as Braelynn threw Olivia the key, Olivia rushed over to Alex and freed her from the cage. Her backpack slipped off her shoulder, and Olivia remembered she had an invention inside that might be able to save Rick.

"Before we leave, I need to make another deal with you." Olivia took out a gold coin from her backpack and showed it to Braelynn. "If I give you this gold coin, you have to promise you won't harm Rick."

Braelynn's eyes widened at the gold, and then she said, "Deal."

Olivia threw the coin to the ground, and it exploded in a burst of smoke.

While all the pirates were coughing and trying to see, Olivia grabbed Rick and they all headed to the end of the cave. It was a dead end.

"Look," Olivia said. "That boulder above us looks like it's another one of the traps." She pointed to a piece of slate with Amanda's business symbol. She stepped on it, and the boulder fell, blocking the pirates' path.

"Um, Olivia," Alex said, "what are these?" She pointed to more pieces of slate along the walls of the cave.

"There's one on each of the walls," Olivia said.

"I want to know what they do," Max said.

"Well then, I hope it's a way to get us out of here," Olivia said, pressing on one of them. Nothing happened. Alex pressed on another one, Max pressed on the third, and Rick pressed on the fourth. Suddenly, the ground beneath them began to lower until it came to a stop in an underground lair. It was dark but lit up in some corners by odd-looking inventions. On one wall, there was a corkboard that looked like a suspect board with pictures, thumbtacks, and string.

They stepped off the rock, and it went back up.

"Where are we?" Max asked.

"Um, guys," Olivia said, pointing to Aunt Amanda.

CHAPTER FIFTEEN

LOOKING FOR REVENGE

"**A**unt Amanda?" Olivia exclaimed.

"You aren't supposed to be here!" Amanda scolded, pointing to Olivia from what looked like her office. "How did you even find me?"

"It depends if you want to be sitting here for hours or not," Olivia said.

"Those stupid pirates were supposed to take care of anyone who entered the cave leading here," Amanda said, making a fist with her one hand. She walked over to them. "Rick? Alex?"

"Long time no see," Rick said.

"You let them escape from my lair," Amanda said. "But none of you will escape from here!"

"It doesn't have to be this way," Olivia's mom said, standing up to her sister.

"You don't understand," Amanda said. "In the past, I would have been dumb and turned my self in, but welcome to the future. I doubt any of you would like to join Sadie," Amanda said, looking at Alex.

"That's it!" Alex said, charging at Amanda. But Olivia stopped her by stepping in front of Alex.

"Alex, I get it," Olivia said, putting her hand on Alex's shoulder. "Just learn to keep it in."

"No, you don't get it!" Alex said, tearing up and

slipping out of Olivia's grasp. "I would do anything to get my mom back."

"I do understand that, but you can't get her back. You have to face that, Alex," Olivia said. "I'm not trying to be rude or anything."

"As much as I love to hear people fight, I still want to know why you're here," Amanda said, getting impatient.

"We all have different reasons," Olivia said.

"Oh yeah? And what are those?" Amanda asked.

"I'm here to find out why you killed my mom," Alex said.

"And I'm here to get my invention notebook back," Olivia said. "The *real* one."

"And I'm here to get revenge for keeping me locked down in that lair for years," Rick said.

"Very funny that you think you can get revenge on me," Amanda said with a laugh. "And why is the annoying brother here, too?"

"What? You have a brother, too? How come you never told me about this, Mom?" Max asked.

"I'm talking about you, dummy!" Amanda said.

"Maybe you *are* a death eater," Max said, crossing his arms and pouting.

"Hold on," Olivia said, grouping together with her family. "I have an idea of how to get my notebook back and get revenge but... Where is Alex?"

Every one started looking around.

"Alex?" Olivia called.

"Alex?" Rick said.

"She has to be somewhere in here," Olivia's mom said.

"You gave me fake gold!" Braelynn said, standing behind them, her face turning red.

"Braelynn?" Olivia asked, turning to face her. "How did you get here and past the rock?" Olivia asked.

"There was a lever on the other side, and I know my way around these caves," Braelynn explained. "And you owe me!" She took out her sword and pointed it at Olivia.

"Don't!" Olivia said. "Please, we need to find Alex."

"I don't care! Just give me real gold!" Braelynn scolded.

"We came here by accident," Olivia said. "You have our money. Isn't that enough?"

"A pirate could never have enough!" Braelynn said.

"We don't have real gold!" Olivia explained. "And we don't have time. We need to find Alex!"

"If she came down here with you, then she must be here somewhere," Braelynn said. "And Amanda couldn't have her because she left right before you came into the cave," Braelynn said.

"No, that's impossible. Amanda is right here with us," Olivia said, starting to look around, but she saw that Amanda was gone. "Where did she go?"

"We must have been so caught up in finding Alex that we didn't realize she escaped," Rick said.

Olivia knew that wherever Amanda was, there was nowhere she wouldn't find her.

CHAPTER SIXTEEN

TRADING TRICKS

"**A**manda must have Alex," Olivia said. "But they couldn't have snuck past us, could they?" Rick asked.

"No clue, unless they're still here," Olivia said.

"Um, it is possible that they could still be here," Max said.

"And right you are," Amanda said with an evil grin on her face as she walked out from a hallway next to her office.

"Amanda, what did you do with Alex?" Olivia's mom asked.

"Don't worry. I didn't harm her. She's right here," Amanda said, gesturing to Alex, who was coming up behind her.

Alex stepped in front of Amanda, and Amanda put her hands on Alex's shoulders.

"Alex, what's going on?" Olivia asked.

"Olivia, I'll explain later."

"There will be no later. You take them to the jail cells this instant," Amanda said.

"You can't boss Alex around like that," Olivia said.

"Oh, but yes, I can," Amanda replied. "You see Alex wanted her mother, and so I made a little deal with her."

"Wait. What? How can you make a deal with her if her mom is dead?" Olivia asked.

Alex started walking over to Olivia and her family. "Come on. You're coming with me."

"What deal did you make?" Olivia asked.

"It's none of your business," Amanda said. "Alex, do as you were told."

"I'm really sorry, Olivia, but you have to come with me," Alex said.

"I trusted you," Olivia said. "But you just lured me here, didn't you?"

"Olivia, you don't understand. I have to."

"No you don't, Alex. For all I know right now, you were only pretending to be my friend."

"Let's go," Alex said, pulling Olivia toward the hallway.

"Alex, save yourself some time. Here are hand-cuffs," Amanda said, taking some out of her desk drawer. "After being arrested so many times, I have a lot of these now because I stole them for evil matters." Amanda threw the handcuffs and a pair of keys to Alex.

"What are they keys for?" Olivia said.

"They better be to free us," Max said.

"Max, why would she handcuff us and then unhandcuff us?

"Don't ask me questions I don't know how to answer."

"Whatever," Olivia said, rolling her eyes.

"And make it quick," Amanda said, pointing toward the hall.

"Huh?" Olivia asked, watching Alex head down the hall. "Where is she going?"

"She gets her half of the deal first. I figure she'll trust me more then," Amanda said.

"Who would ever trust you?" Olivia asked.

"Apparently your cousin," Amanda said with a chuckle.

Alex walked out from the hallway with a woman following her. The woman had messy red hair and was wearing ripped shorts and a faded T-shirt.

"Who's that?" Olivia asked.

"It couldn't be," Olivia's mom said, staring at the woman.

"Olivia, this is my mom," Alex said. "When I found out she was alive and Amanda was holding her hostage, I made the deal with Amanda that I'd work for her if she gave me my mom back. I'm really sorry. I should have told you sooner, but I was afraid Amanda would go back on the deal."

"Alex, I get it. She's your mom. I'd do the same thing."

"Yeah, yeah, yeah. Hurry up and put the handcuffs on them already, Alex. It's time for you to give me my half of the deal," Amanda said.

Alex walked over to Olivia and winked at her before trying to put the handcuffs on her. Olivia slid back, but Alex got around her and slid them on her wrists. Olivia noticed that the handcuffs weren't really locked. Maybe her cousin wasn't really going to help Amanda after all. Olivia saw Alex tilt her head toward Olivia's hands to show the others so they'd let her put the handcuffs on them, too. After Alex had pretended to handcuff everyone, Ashley popped up from around the corner of the hallway.

"Alex, you didn't have to do that," Ashley said.

"What? Why?" Alex said.

Amanda started laughing.

"I made that same deal with Amanda. That's why I tried to get away from you all before. I didn't want you coming here and getting involved. But she tricked us."

"You fools will never learn," Amanda said. She walked over to Olivia's mom. "Looks like your family will never win."

"You're wrong," Olivia's mom said. "I reported you to the police. They'll be after you."

"Please. They won't find me. I've escaped from them numerous times. I doubt they'd finally get me."

"Maybe you're wrong," Olivia said.

"What? I'm never wrong. I have everything I want, and now I have two new people working for me." Amanda turned and looked at Braelynn. "Soon, I'll have you and your crew as well."

Braelynn aimed her sword at Amanda.

"You wouldn't dare," Amanda said.

Braelynn backed down. Olivia couldn't believe that Braelynn would actually give in.

"Amanda, this isn't right. It doesn't have to be this way. Wouldn't you like a break from being evil? You can still rule this place if you want to, but you don't have to make everyone miserable. You don't have to trap them here. And you don't have to do this to us," Olivia said.

Amanda walked over to Olivia. "Oh, and what are you going to do?" she asked, going to put her hands on Olivia's shoulders. But Olivia grabbed her handcuffs and put them on Amanda's wrists.

Alex high-fived Olivia as the others all dropped their handcuffs.

Amanda screamed and lunged at Olivia. Braelynn put her sword out in front of Amanda. "I don't think so," Braelynn said. "We're all done taking orders from you."

"What? You can't do this to me. I get you most of your gold."

"Gold or no gold, it's better than having you as a ruler," Braelynn said.

Soon, the police stepped off of the elevator with Zane. "I had to," Zane said. "They said they wouldn't arrest us, too, if we helped them catch Amanda."

"That was actually great timing," Braelynn said.

"She's over here," Olivia said.

"I see you've already gotten this under control," the police officer said, motioning to the handcuffs on Amanda's wrists. "Thank you for your help," the officer said.

"No, thank you. We've been through a lot of trouble with her," Olivia said.

"Have a nice rest of your vacation," the officer said, taking Amanda away.

Alex reached into her back pocket and took out Olivia's invention notebook. "I found this when I was freeing my mom. I figured you might want it back."

Olivia took the notebook and hugged Alex. "Thank you so much!" Olivia said.

"Maybe it's time we stop being pirates and give

all these people the freedom they deserve by being their new rulers," Braelynn said.

"That wouldn't be bad," Zane said. "King Zane has a nice ring to it."

"Oh man, *I* wanted to be king," Max said.

"Max, if you can discover your own land, then sure, you can be king of it," Olivia said.

"What happens now?" Alex asked.

"I'd say we all deserve a vacation after this. A *real* vacation to get to know our family members, Ashley, Sadie, Alex..." Olivia saw Rick lower his head. "And Rick," she added.

"Wait. We're related to Rick, too?" Max asked.

Olivia smiled at Rick. "I'd say he's family now."

"I think this calls for gelato on the beach back at Abura with Grandma and Grandpa, too," Max said.

Olivia patted Max on the head. "Max, I think that's the best idea you've ever had."

The End

ALSO BY AYLA HASHWAY

The Secret Sister

ACKNOWLEDGMENTS

I'd like to thank my mom for encouraging me to write more often and also write my first books. I'd also like to thank my grandparents for taking me to Aruba and inspiring me in so many different ways. Thank you to everyone who read *The Secret Sister* and asked me to write another book about Olivia and Max.

ABOUT THE AUTHOR

Ayla Hashway is ten years old. She loves reading and writing. *The Lost Island* is her second book, although she's been writing for years. She believes if you keep trying, you can make your dreams come true.

For more information, check out Ayla's blog:
https://readingwritinglovinglife.blogspot.com

Printed in Great Britain
by Amazon